ETHEL'S SONG

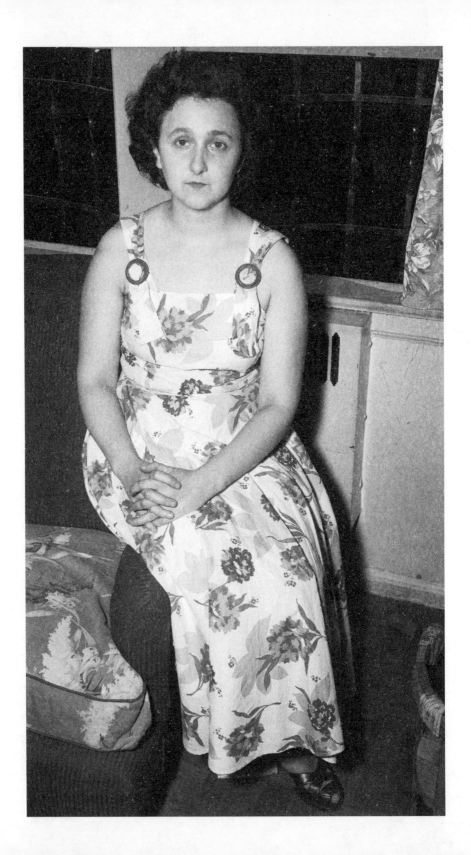

ETHEL'S SONG

ETHEL ROSENBERG'S LIFE IN POEMS

A NOVEL IN VERSE BY
BARBARA KRASNER

CALKINS CREEK
AN IMPRINT OF ASTRA BOOKS FOR YOUNG READERS
New York

For my late parents, Milton and Lillian Perlman Krasner

For information about permission to reproduce selections from this book,
please contact permissions@astrapublishinghouse.com.

Calkins Creek
An imprint of Astra Books for Young Readers, a division of Astra Publishing House
astrapublishinghouse.com
Printed in the United States of America

ISBN: 978-1-63592-625-5 (hc)
ISBN: 978-1-63592-626-2 (eBook)
Library of Congress Cataloging-in-Publication Data
Names: Krasner, Barbara, author.
Title: Ethel's song : Ethel Rosenberg's life in poems / Barbara Krasner.
Description: First edition. | New York : Calkins Creek, an imprint of Astra Books for
young readers, [2022] | Includes bibliographical references. |Audience: Ages 13-17 |
Audience: Grades 10-12 | Summary: "In 1953, Ethel Rosenberg, a devoted wife and
loving mother, faces the electric chair. People say she's a spy, a Communist, a traitor, a
red. How did she get here? In a series of heart-wrenching poems, Ethel tells her story.
The child of Jewish immigrants, Ethel Greenglass grows up on New York City's Lower
East Side. She dreams of being an actress and a singer but finds romance and excitement
in the arms of the charming Julius Rosenberg. Both are ardent supporters of rights for
workers, but are they spies? Who is passing atomic secrets to the Soviets? Why does
everyone seem out to get them? This first book for young readers about Ethel
Rosenberg is a fascinating portrait of a commonly misunderstood figure from American
history, and vividly relates a story that continues to have relevance today."— Provided
by publisher. Identifiers: LCCN 2022004253 (print) | LCCN 2022004254 (ebook) |
ISBN 9781635926255 (hardcover) | ISBN 9781635926262 (epub)
Subjects: LCSH: Rosenberg, Ethel, 1915-1953--Juvenile poetry.
Classification: LCC HX84.R578 K73 2022 (print) | LCC HX84.R578 (ebook) |
DDC 364.1/31092 [B]--dc23/eng/20220321
LC record available at https://lccn.loc.gov/2022004253
LC ebook record available at https://lccn.loc.gov/2022004254

First edition
10 9 8 7 6 5 4 3 2 1

Design by Barbara Grzeslo
The text is set in Sabon.
The titles are set in Impact.

Frontispiece:
Ethel Rosenberg in her apartment the day after husband Julius's arrest, July 1950

CONTENTS

PART I | Sheriff Street   9

PART II | Knickerbocker Village   89

PART III | Federal Courthouse, Foley Square   177

PART IV | Sing Sing Federal Prison, Ossining, New York   199

EPILOGUE   247

AUTHOR'S NOTE   252

ACKNOWLEDGMENTS   253

TIMELINE OF EVENTS   254

SOURCE NOTES   260

SELECTED BIBLIOGRAPHY   264

FOR MORE INFORMATION   269

PICTURE CREDITS   271

PART I | SHERIFF STREET

WHAT IT MEANS TO BE A GIRL
1925

Wash out your baby brother's diapers,
darn your oldest brother's socks,
slip from your middle brother's wrestling holds.

Most of all, stay out of Mama's way.
Her tongue whacks like a leather belt
catching on my ten-year-old confidence.

Some girls may place their ambitions
in hope chests. But here on Sheriff
Street, here in the tenements

of New York City's Lower East Side,
we children of immigrants sweep them
under the beds like dust.

SWEET DREAMS

At night, when the apartment is still,
I pull my dreams from under the bed—
each one I savor, bend to my will.

I'm an actress, an audience thrill.
The world is my stage, my lines well read,
at night, when the apartment is still.

A singer am I, soprano trill,
high octave notes, they dance, well led—
each one I savor, bend to my will.

Photographers greet me, frame with skill,
reporters quote me with pencil lead
at night, when the apartment is still.

My clothes are gold, my heavy purse filled
with money enough to turn my head—
each buck I savor, bend to my will.

One day, just see, my dreams will instill
sweet fortunes, and love will bring me bread
at night, when the apartment is still—
each dream I savor, bend to my will.

NUMBER 64

In a nondescript tenement
on a nondescript street,
we live behind Papa's sewing machine
repair shop. He bends over his machine
as poverty bends over us.

Machine shops line the street
like tight stitches in a seam,
leaning on each other
to make a single straight pattern of income.

OUT ON THE STREET

My mother is a terror
since she became a bill collector,
dragging along my brother Bernie
because he can rough up deadbeats.

My mother is an embarrassment
dragging her shopping bag,
looking for bargains,
haggling with pushcart vendors
as if she were still in the shtetl.

My mother is a thief,
dragging my stolen dreams
through the mud, stomping
on them with her thick, unlaced boots.

HALF A SIBLING

Half a sibling is Sammy.
Whole is the bitterness of Sammy
that makes the six years between us
a gaping hole.
Just because I'm the only girl
and Papa adores me.

MOVING ON UP

Mama must have haggled a good deal.
Papa's business must be doing well.
Mama rents an upstairs apartment
so she, Papa, and Sammy
can spread out
in the ground-floor flat.
Bernie, two years younger,
little Dovey, six years younger,
and I move up.
Mama's tongue lashings
refuse to climb stairs.
Mama's broad swipes
slip on the stairwell.
Mama's heavy footsteps
remain grounded.
Up here I have my own room,
a window looking out onto the street,
sunlight and air.

THE DICTIONARY PLAN

I decide to increase
my vocabulary
by learning one new
word
a day.

Today's
word:
Exigency—
A situation that demands remedy.
The bare icebox,
shoes from two years ago that pinch,
the greengrocer's constant pleas to pay the bill.
Now our gnawing needs
fit within the boundaries
of just one ever-widening word:
Exigency.

DOVEY

I love to poke my fingers
through little Dovey's curls.

I love to tickle his tummy
and hear his laughter.

I love this brother so dearly
because he obeys me.

STITCHES

Implacable—
Not to be
pacified.

Put it in a sentence:
I am implacable
when it comes
to fights
with Mama.

I love Papa,
but he uses all
his strength
in his mechanical repairs.
There's none left
for his words.

WHEN I SING, WHEN I ACT

I become anyone I want.
I go anywhere I please.
I say anything that comes to me.
I make words dance.

When I sing, when I act,
I am in charge, I make the rules.
I rise above this ugly Lower East Side,
the tenement buildings
        that fold into each other,
The Yiddish babble
        of fish for sale.

On stage with an opera company,
I am Barbarina, singing soprano
in Mozart's *Marriage of Figaro*.
After my aria, audiences erupt
in rambunctious applause.
On stage with a repertory troupe,
I am Ophelia in Shakespeare's *Hamlet*.
Audiences detonate in waves of cheers.
They say, "Boy, can she act? And how!"

THE WALK TO
SEWARD PARK HIGH SCHOOL
1928

I shuffle to school
with paper stuck

inside my shoes
to hide the holes

in the soles, to cushion me
from cracks in concrete sidewalk.

WHERE THERE'S A WORD

My English teacher tells me
I possess a laudable
vocabulary.

College, here I come!

ETHEL'S FOUR QUESTIONS

As a girl, and because I'm not the youngest,
I don't get to ask the Four Questions
at the Passover Seder. I don't get to ask:
Why is this night different from other nights?
Why do we usually eat leavened bread but tonight we eat matzo?
Why do we usually eat vegetables but tonight we eat bitter herbs?
Why do we usually sit up straight but tonight we recline?

My own questions aren't specific to Passover:
Why does a government allow its people to live in such poverty?
Why can't we all believe in whatever makes sense to us?
Why must there be hate in the world?
Why must there be war?

THE SEWARD PARK HIGH SCHOOL *ALMANAC*

1931

Best Actress:
Ethel Greenglass
Class Prophecy:
By 1950, Ethel Greenglass
will become a celebrity.
From the pages of the Seward Park *Almanac*
to G-d's ear.

The next time Mama covers her ears
when I sing, I'll sing even louder.

Ethel Greenglass graduates from
Seward Park High School, 1931.

NEEDLESS NEEDLES

For two years now,
since the stock market crashed
down on Wall Street,
we've been plunged
into a great Depression.
Nobody needs the work
of our tailors and seamstresses,
patternmakers and pressers
in the uptown Garment District.
Papa says we'll make do.

President Hoover lies when he says
prosperity is just around the corner.
I can't stand people who lie.

SHIM-SHAM SAMMY

Sammy is only my half-brother,
the product of Papa's
first wife, who died. Sammy married
and moved out. Mama counted
on his rent money. Now as the next oldest,
at sixteen,
I have to make up the difference.
"Get a job,"
Mama says. "But I was going
to act! I was going to sing! I
was going to go to college!" I say.
"Get your head out of the clouds,
girl. The whole country's in a depression,
and you're selfish, thinking only of yourself."
Is it wrong, am I offending G-d
by disliking my mother so much?

SO MUCH FOR COLLEGE
1932

Wanted!
Unskilled workers
at the
National New York Packaging and Shipping Company.

Wanted!
A queue of people wants
the same job, my job.

Wanted!
The crowd gets unruly,
people shove and shout.
The police force them
under control with a hose.

Wanted!
Not me.
I sign up
for a six-month secretarial course.
I earn my certificate in typing,
bookkeeping, stenography.

Wanted!
Me!
I'm the new clerk
at the
National New York Packaging and Shipping Company
uptown in the Garment District.

Wanted!
People like me—
young, fast, eager.
Yet who am I at sixteen, when so many thousands
are out of work, to find work so quickly?
Am I in the right place
at the right time?
Or am I just willing to work
for such low wages?

BEYOND THE LOWER EAST SIDE

I nudge
my way onto the M train
to Herald Square. As we worm
through Manhattan's underbelly,
soot and silt
and impossibilities
fall away.

On the job, I meet Jews
from the Bronx and New Jersey. I
meet Italians and other Catholics.
"How ya doin'?"
"*Buon giorno!*"
Nobody asks where I'm from.
Nobody asks about my family.
Nobody asks about high school.
Just "How fast can you type?"

I sharpen my pencils.
I roll a piece of paper
into the typewriter.
"120 words a minute," I say,
"without looking."

IF I HAD A MAP

I'd have to increase the size of Japan
to include Manchuria,
pardon me, Manchukuo,
Japan's new economy builder.

I'd have to increase the sphere
of Japan to include Shanghai
and let's not forget Korea,
under Japanese influence for decades.

If I had a map,
I'd see Japan as a
country gobbler.

MY DEEP, DARK SECRET

I know I should buy
at Woolworth's five-and-dime, but
they don't have the right lipstick shade.

So I scan the newspaper ads
until I find a sale
at Lord & Taylor.

I have my choices:
Light Rose, Raspberry,
Pomegranate, Orange,

but I choose Bright Red
and follow the natural lines
of my own lips.

ONE DAY, ALL DAYS AT NATIONAL

Timecard in
Punch the clock
Position the fingers
Index fingers on F and J
Middle fingers on D and K
Ring fingers on S and L
Pinkies on A and semicolon
Thumbs ready to hit space
Type
Type
Type
Bell rings
Timecard in
Punch.

FRANKLIN DELANO ROOSEVELT
1933

Hoover out
Roosevelt in

Republicans out
Democrats in

Lies out
Hope in

Roosevelt's New Deal promises jobs
to build roads and parks, plant trees.

Those jobs are for men,
those jobs take them far from home.

We need jobs right here
in New York. All of us.

Who can help us
on the Lower East Side?

LET'S GET DOWN TO WORK

The Communist Party says
we all need to get down to work.
Protest unemployment!
Demand relief if you don't
have a job!

Strike!
To get what you need!
Strike!
To get what you deserve!

Madison Square Garden
fills with those of us
who are tired
of rich politicians
telling us things will be better.

Even the *Jewish Daily Forward*,
Papa's favorite paper,
is always on the side of the worker.

A NEW CIRCLE

My friends and I
gather round the piano
in someone's apartment.
I'm eager to sing.
I want to sing.
I demand to sing.
My notes swirl around the room,
twirl around my vocal chords.
We're not looking for revolution
at these Young Communist League
clubs. We're looking
to entertain,
bring the arts to the people.
We are a fraternity
of musicians
artists
singers
circulating through New York City,
dropping ringlets of culture
to anyone who wants them.

A NEW WORD FOR MY DICTIONARY

Everyone's talking
of a word I've not heard
before:
Fascism.

A government with a dictator
A government that takes total control
A government with troops in brown shirts
who beat up ordinary people.
A place where it's not safe to say
what you think.
A place where the government gets rid of people
it doesn't like.

Benito Mussolini controls Italy.
Adolf Hitler controls Germany.
Who and what are next?

WOMEN DEMAND MORE
1935

Three years on the job,
I join the Ladies Apparel Shipping Clerks
Union. "We demand a 35-hour workweek!"
"We insist on $23 a week, not 14!"
Fifteen thousand voices in solidarity!

I complain about the pay. But instead
of an increase, I'm told—
You make too many mistakes in your
Shorthand
Typing
Filing.

The hairs
at the back of my head bristle. I know
that's not true. It's a ruse to shut me, us,
down.

Mama's voice echoes in my head.
Not good enough
Not good enough
Not good enough.

TAKING IT UPSTAIRS

We're going to strike!
I escort the committee members

to my bedroom
and slam the door
past Mama's mumblings.

THE DAY OF THE TRUCKS

One woman organizes about 150 of us
into squads. I help form a squad
right outside the building where we work.

The mission is clear: Stop the delivery trucks.
We splay ourselves on asphalt
We wear bravado over our raincoats
We fill the street with our bodies.

Hey, Mr. Truck Driver,
you want to get through?
You're going to have to drive
over us.

I close my eyes. All I hear
is the idled anger of motors.
I sing to myself. August sweat creases
my dress.

They won't dare
They won't dare
They don't dare.

SCUM

The street is silent
as I walk with friends
after a strikers meeting
at Christ Church on West 36th Street
in Hell's Kitchen. Out of shadows
half a block away come ten men
with iron pipes.
They swing at us,
flesh-pounding
bone-crushing
swings. I drop to the street,
unharmed.
The shadows disappear leaving
writhing, screaming, bloodied bodies
in the shimmering cobblestone street.
Strikers rush to their aid. I watch,
unable to move, unable to speak.

IN THE NEWS

National New York Packaging and Shipping Company
hired thugs
to beat us, to stop our strike.
News agencies splash us on print pages.

It's right to stand up for what you believe in.
It's right to call out injustices.
It's right to commit yourself to the fight.

More, I want more!
More union meetings on my calendar!
More picket signs!

STRIKEOVER

After ten days, the strike ends without much
gain. One by one, strike committee members
are fired—including
me.

THE CANARY SINGS

Sing!
When there's no work to be had.

Sing!
To audition for the Schola Cantorum—
the citywide choir.
I learned how to play piano for this.
I learned how to sight-read music for this.

Sing!
I make the cut!

Now our chorus of 200 voices
lifts up the audience
with the music of the
New York Philharmonic
at Carnegie Hall.

Sing!
To the balcony
To the mezzanine.
Open those vocal chords,
throttle for Toscanini.

Sing!
When you sing at Carnegie Hall,
even at nineteen,
you've made it!

This choir is just the first step
for Ethel Greenglass.

THE PEALING OF A NEW BELL
1936

Who knew that I could get
a stenographer job for more money
and fewer hours? Thank you,
Bell Textile Company.

It's near City Hall so I can hoof it
and not waste my money on the subway.
Soon I will
be able to afford voice lessons.
Hallelujah!
I bring lunch on challah.

AT CARNEGIE HALL STUDIOS

Ooh-la-la!
The phonograph needle hits the grooves of
flutes and piccolos,
violins and cellos,
trumpets and drums
while Madame plays piano keys.

Ooh-la-la!
My mouth opens so wide,
my chin hits my chest,
my lips quiver as I hold
the exaggerated notes
of operetta composers
Victor Herbert and Sigmund Romberg.

Ooh-la-la!
I wear a hoop-skirted costume,
a velvet-trimmed hat,
I am operatic film star Jeanette MacDonald
in *Naughty Marietta*, svelte and blond.

Only I'm not.
Two dollars per lesson come out
of my purse into Madame's pocket.

SONG FOR THE PICKET LINE

Every Saturday, Ohrbach's
department store workers carry signs

Unfair labor!
On strike against meager wages

against increased working hours
at the same pay

outside its department store
on East 14th Street.

Every Saturday, Ohrbach's
workers hope they can make a difference.

Every Saturday, people
think workers standing up for their rights

is a bad thing. They hurl
Communist labels at workers.

Every Saturday people yell,
"Marxists!" "Reds!" at the workers.

Every Saturday is Ohrbach's
Day when police arrest the workers

but this July Saturday
I serenade the picketers:

Don't despair!
Carry on!

THE G-MEN

A newly named agency—
the Federal Bureau of Investigation—
is on a mission to wipe out gangsters
with its G-men. Bank robberies have been cut
in half, the *New York Times* says. The G-men
have won convictions in nearly all cases.

Everywhere
there's a G-man, trench coat flapping
in the wind of truth, justice, and the American way.

Solved fifty kidnapping cases,
broken up notorious gangs of criminals,
sent twenty-five big-time public enemies to prison.

The proud papa, FBI chief
J. Edgar Hoover,
is quoted and pictured daily.

But I don't trust a man with
a crooked mouth.

CIVIL WAR IN SPAIN
JULY 1936

The streets and papers buzz with news—
an uprising
against the government
in favor of a fascist dictator
who'll control everything in Spain.

The Communist Party
here in New York wants to run programs
and raise money to fight this rebellion,
keep the government in place.
Fascism is worse than capitalism, they say.
If we don't help to fight it, if we don't help
the Soviet Union fight against fascism,
America will be next.

I volunteer. Thousands of us volunteer.
Tens of thousands of us support
the Communist Party USA,
the Spanish government,
and antifascism.

THE SIT-INS

Only the Communist Party
is willing to take a stand—
Against fascism
Against social injustice
Against unemployment.

Its Workers Alliance
calls for sit-ins
in
Brooklyn
Harlem
Manhattan
to demand more relief for the unemployed.

Someone from the Alliance
escorts me from sit-in to sit-in
from dusk to dawn.
"Here's your entertainment," he says
as he introduces me
to sit-in groups of hundreds
of men, women, and children,
restless protesters.

I spend the night singing Italian arias.
On my entrance, the halls,
the walls whisper "Ethel."
On my exit,
they scream, "Encore!"

NEW CHINESE FORTUNE
NOVEMBER 1936

I decide to splurge on a Chinese lunch,
but the waiter forgets to bring me
my sweet-and-sour chicken.

My waiter announces: New fortune today.
"There is no rose without a thorn."
He throws fortune cookies on the table.

The rose: China has been getting ammunitions
from the Soviet Union to stave off
Japanese invasion.

The thorn: Today Germany and Japan
signed a five-year pact against
the Soviet Union.

The waiter delivers my chicken,
but it tastes only sour.

THE SEAMEN'S BENEFIT
DECEMBER 1936

I accept a request to sing at a benefit
for the union of fishermen.

A young man approaches as if
he had parted the Red Sea just to see me.

"You come here often?" he asks in tenor voice.
"I'm the entertainment," I say.

"I've seen you before."
"Really?"

"The Ohrbach's strike? I picketed."
"I sang to the picketers."

He breaks into a beguiling smile.
"That must be it."

"Name's Julius, Julius Rosenberg."
We shake hands. He already knows

my name from the evening's
Master of Ceremonies.

       I curl his name
       on my tongue,   J-u-l-i-u-s

I take the stage;
I am under a sorcerer's spell.

CIRIBIRIBIN (from the Italian love song)

Ah, Ciribiribin, it's you I love.
Your easy smile, arresting gray-green eyes.
Sweet violins bring me to you, my dove.

You're my tenacious tenor, strong and tough.
I'm your soprano, shy, petite in size.
Ah, Ciribiribin, it's you I love.

The room is crowded, chandelier above.
Sheer voltage sparks—you, me—now energized.
Sweet violins bring me to you, my dove.

With each *r* I trill, your name is a glove.
You're Rosenberg, Julius, heart's sunrise.
Ah, Ciribiribin, it's you I love.

Notes climb the narrow streets and blindman's bluff.
They plummet, they glide to valleys nearby.
Sweet violins bring me to you, my dove.

You stand before me, vulnerable scruff.
I stand before you, redeemable prize.
Sweet violins bring me to you, my dove.
Ah, Ciribiribin, it's you I love.

COLLEGE MAN

"I'm a sophomore
      at City College," he tells me.
I've never known a college man.
      "Engineering."

We're far away from the stage,
      but the light remains in his eyes.

"I don't know if I should tell you this,"
he whispers. "But somehow,
I feel like we've always
      known each other."

      Is he a hypnotist?
      He reels me in like river carp.

"What do you want to tell me?
I can keep secrets."

His eyes dart from left to right
like a metronome.

"I've made an important decision.
I've joined a club at school."

"Well, that's nothing to hide," I say.
"What club?"

"The Young Communist League. We
want to change the world,
make things better
for the worker, for everyone."

"Ethel," somebody says,
"Your mother's going to kill you,
it's so late!" I glance at my watch.
Oy gevalt, she's right. "My coat!
"I've got to go!"

He rushes to get it for me.
"May I take you home?" he asks.

It may be winter,
but I feel
only warmth.

A DATE WITH JULIE

We've neither of us money
No dinner out
No movie night
We take the subway
to Coney Island
Walk the sands
Shoes in one hand
Interlaced fingers
Interlaced thoughts of a world without poverty.

NIGHTS

Julie skirts past Mama's apartment
to get to me upstairs.
He studies, books splayed on the table.
I type his papers, correcting as I go.

Some nights we go to Times Square.
Julie presses his hand into mine and says,
"Sing, dearest! I love to hear your voice!"
I sing for the defeat of fascists in Spain,
I sing for the oppressed,
I sing "Tango of the Roses" for Julie.

MEETING JULIE'S FAMILY

A man brings home his girlfriend
to meet his parents? This is serious business.

Julie's parents are immigrants
from eastern Europe like my parents.

But Julie's father stands tall with the success
of protesting for workers' rights.

Julie's mother holds my hands
the way she holds on to good fortune.

Julie's brother, Dave, raises his glass
the way he's raised himself with a Columbia College scholarship.

Julie's sisters—Lena, Ethel, and Ida—
serve and clean up, not expecting the college life.

Like traditional immigrant Jewish families,
on Julie, the youngest, they all place

their dreams of greatness.
"Mark my words," his father says,

"Julius will be a *makher*, a somebody."
I think so too.

THE FOUR QUESTIONS REVISITED
1937

Why does a government allow its people to live in poverty?
>Not all governments allow this. Look at Russia.

Why can't we just believe in what makes sense to us?
>The Republicans don't make sense.
>The Democrats (sorry, Mr. President) don't make sense.
>The Communist Party matches what I believe in.

Why must there be hate?
>We hate what we don't understand.
>We hate people we don't understand.

Why must there be war?
>I can't answer this one.

THREE LITTLE PIGS

Once upon a time,
there were three little pigs.

The first little pig—Japan—
took bites of China and Korea,
Manchuria too,
and demanded more.

The second little pig—Italy—
munched on Ethiopia and Libya
and was still hungry.

The third little pig—Germany—
gorged on Austria, Bohemia, Moravia,
France, the Netherlands,
Luxembourg, Belgium,
and was still ravenous.

They all signed a treaty to protect
each other if attacked,
wee-wee-wee, all the way home.

DOVEY JOINS THE YOUNG COMMUNIST LEAGUE
1938

Watching Julie with Dovey, now sixteen,
I imagine Julie
as the father of our own child some day.

He helps Dovey learn engineering.
He gives him a slide rule.
He shares Communist pamphlets and books.

Dovey joins the Young Communist League.
One of 12,000 members in New York City,
he learns the teachings of Karl Marx,
that all workers should unite
to fight against big bosses.
He learns it's his responsibility to ease
the struggles of the American worker.

A GREENGLASS CIVIL WAR

Civil war rages in Spain
and on Sheriff Street.
My half-brother Sammy
has always resented me.
For him I had to give up my college dream
and get a job.
I've never forgiven him.

Sammy says,
"I hate you Communists.
You're destroying America.
Just because all the Russians
are now Communists, it doesn't
mean we need that here!
You want to be Communists?
Fine, I'll give you the money.
Go to Russia and stay there."

Sammy says. "I don't like
how you're filling
Dovey's head with this filth."
"It's not filth," Julie says.
"It's the way to a better life.
A life where everyone can benefit."

Sammy says, "Communists don't belong
in America. Not in my America." He
heads for the door and turns back,
stares Julie and me in the face.
"I never want to see the two of you again."

I could live with that.

TOGETHER

I long to see Julie now
  Every day
How strong I'll be with Julie now
  In every way
Nothing's wrong, I'm with Julie now
  No matter what they say
It won't be long, forever with Julie now
  He's here to stay.

WAIT

"I'll work all the days of my life," I say
to Julie. I want to marry now.

But he holds firm. "No, no wife
of mine will work."

Even his father agrees: What's the harm in waiting?
Julie will graduate and get a good job.

Each night our lips break apart,
each night our hands let go

The braided string between us still firm
like the cables of the Brooklyn Bridge.

A DIFFERENT KIND OF CAMP
NOVEMBER 1938

Who knew that Nazi Germany was invading
its own country, imprisoning
Jews in concentration camps during a
two-day raid in November?

Who knew that 7,000 Jews were just released
from Dachau and Buchenwald
on the condition they leave Germany?

I always wanted to escape the city
and go to a camp where I could breathe
fresh air, sing to mountaintops.

But 7,000 Jews
had their heads shaved, were starved,
and developed frostbite at Dachau and Buchenwald.

HITLER HELPS HIMSELF
1938–1939

Fascism also means
invading other countries
and announcing to the world
they belong to you.

Hitler has invaded
the Sudetenland
Hitler has annexed
Austria
Hitler has marched
on Czechoslovakia.

I'm almost scared to read
a newspaper these days.
I'm grateful for Julie,
keeping me strong
against Hitler.

LOVE IS

Love is defying my mother
and bringing Julie to my room

Love is accepting and giving
compliments, sincerely meant

Love is sharing world views
and wanting to put the world right

Love is typing Julie's college notes
and papers so he can focus

on his classes and
Young Communist League meetings.

LET'S GET MARRIED

"Let's get married," Julie
says. "It's the only way

to see each other every day.
We don't need much fanfare.

A simple wedding in the rabbi's study.
A few close friends and family.

On Sunday, June 18, 1939,
Julie takes my hand in his.

He stomps the napkin-wrapped glass
and everyone shouts, "Mazel tov!"

Congratulations, Mr. and Mrs. Julius Rosenberg.
I am now his honey wife.

OUR HONEYMOON

"Why don't you come with us
to the Catskills?" Julie's sister
asks. This trip
could be the honeymoon
we never had.

We rent a cottage in Spring Glen.
Arm in arm we roam the countryside,
the graveled roads lined
with lilacs and sunflowers,
their scent lacing the air.
We stop at the gas station
for a bottle of ice-cold Coca-Cola.
We take turns sipping.
I sing to my husband
in the cool early evening.
Crickets are the chorus.
Julius, my Julie, the song.

INVASION

The fascists are coming
The brown shirts
The beatings
The shootings
They won't care how we struggle
They want to see us crawl
No one, no thing is private
The fragments of our lives will be
controlled by others.

The fascists are coming.
We'll be put in cages
with no chance of survival.
The new gods are coming
with whips and guns,
fire in their bellies,
blackened tongues.
Their blackened eyes
can see the whole moon
and we cannot.

The fascists are coming.
Only the Communists stand
against them. This is our only chance.
Father Joe, Josef Stalin,
Premier of the Soviet state,
leader of the Communist Party.
You are out there on your own
to face the enemy.

THE HANDSHAKE
AUGUST 1939

Mussolini is a dictator.
Hitler is a dictator.

We thought Stalin's Soviet Union
would protect the world,

but now the news in the paper and radio
leave us gasping:

Germany and the Soviet Union
will not invade each other.

Germany and the Soviet Union
will each invade Poland and own a half

like slices of noodle pudding.
Now Nazism is no longer fascist,

Hitler no longer the enemy. Stalin
has given up the fight against fascism.

We wait for some response
from the American Communist Party.

A day, two days, a week, two weeks.
A month, two months.

Finally, the Party makes a statement:
Support the new pact, it's good for world peace.

England and France, now they're supreme capitalists
and Roosevelt is a warmonger!

This turnaround makes no sense.
Do we walk away?

I bite my nails figuring out what to do.
I don't even want to sing right now.

"We'll follow the Party," Julie says.
"We'll show our loyalty."

WAR!

SEPTEMBER 1, 1939

With tanks and planes
Germany invades Poland.

Allies Britain and France
declare war against Germany.

My voice is taken up with words
of war, of tanks and troops.

Roosevelt says America will be neutral,
but he wants to support Britain and France

with war supplies. Doesn't he see
war never solves anything?

The Communist Party has called for a rally
to protest the war at Madison Square Garden.

Julie and I navigate the crowd
and find seats.

Two weeks later, the Soviet Union
invades eastern Poland. It's in the war now,
on the side of Germany.

FROM CLEVER TO COMMANDING

Julie masterminds a list of college friends
he thinks have special technical expertise and can be trusted.
He skillfully discusses the Party's positions
He artfully argues the benefits of Party membership
He proficiently plans meetings, organizes lists.

Julie's graduated from the junior ranks
of the Young Communist League to a full-fledged
member of the Communist Party.
The apprentice is now a master.

THE LADIES' SECTION

We move from the Lower East Side
to Brooklyn
and share the four-room
apartment of friends.

No more tensions,
no more parents.
Just conversation with other smart people,
Communist Party meetings,
fundraisers.

I join the ladies' section of Julie's
engineering trade union. I volunteer
as a typist. As the wives

of union members,
we do what we can to support
our husbands. I form
my opinions quickly. Julie prefers
to listen to what everyone has to say
before coming to his own conclusions.
But when he talks,
all conversation stops. When
Julie asks someone to do something,
it gets done. When Julie recruits,
people ask where to sign. When
Julie says, "Honey wife," I
come to him.

SIGN HERE, PLEASE

A knock at the door
and a woman asks
for signatures on a petition.

A knock at the door
to support a Communist Party
candidate for city council.

I scribble my name.
I don't even know
the candidate's name.

EVERYONE'S DOING IT
1940

Someone's got to be the breadwinner.
Julie and I both wish it would be him.

"I'm taking the Civil Service Exam,"
Julie announces one day.

He says, "The government's hiring
junior engineers."

Just in case things don't work out,
I take the exam too.

I use my maiden name and my parents' address.
Single women have better chances of getting work.

I'm the first to get a job offer in Washington, DC.
"A clerk with the U.S. Census Bureau," I tell Julie.

He tries to be happy for me. He says, "We'll move
to Washington. We can't turn down the money."

I want so much for him to get
a job. When he does, we can

have a bright future even if it's away
from everything and everyone we know.

ONLY A FEW MONTHS

We arrive in Washington in June 1940,
and before the summer ends,

Julie brings news. He's got a job!
It's with the U.S. Signal Corps
as a junior engineer. He'll

inspect electrical equipment
for the U.S. Army.

He has to report for his new job
right after Labor Day, leave

Washington for Fort Monmouth in New Jersey.
Looks like we'll be moving

back to New York City.
"I'll go now," he says,

"and live with my parents." I have
to give notice to the Census Bureau

and must stay another
month without Julie.

But now life will be as it should be.
Julie will be the breadwinner in the family.

THE LIGHT IN JULIE'S EYES

We're back in New York.
Julie's working with fellows
he knew from college.

He's got a light in his eyes.
He's actively recruiting
for the Party and that takes argument.

He's got a gift for it,
learned when he was young
studying Hebrew texts.

He can analyze and present
a conclusion that makes sense.
And that light in his eyes

always tells the truth. Everyone knows
where Julie stands at all times. The light
burns bright when he mentions the Party.

THE DRAFT
OCTOBER 1940

Bernie registers for Selective Service.
I hope his draft number never comes up
or if it does, he won't have to fight.

It's one thing supporting a cause,
supporting faceless masses.
But a brother? I don't want him out there.

At 5'11" and 145 pounds, who knows
how long he'd last? When he shows me
his draft card at dinner, I want to tear it up.

THE HEARING
JANUARY 1941

It comes as a complete surprise
when Julie's employer
calls him in
for a loyalty hearing.

Loyalty! All his overtime,
all his travel, the sacrifices
he's made for that job.

They ask him about
a petition I signed back
in Brooklyn. I don't even
remember it,
that's how important
it was.

Julie gets defiant. "Even if my wife
signed a petition," he says,
"what's that got to do with me? She's
got a right to her own ideas."

But I don't understand. They
had to know Julie's been involved
with the Party since City College. This hearing
is all my fault. Why did I sign
a stupid petition?

YOU WANT LOYALTY?

Julie now knows he has to watch
what he says and where.

But that doesn't stop him
from advocating for other workers.
He takes the helm of the local
union for his coworkers.

He argues for higher wages for overtime
He insists on more training
He demands compensation for travel
between work sites
He fights to get engineers their jobs back
when fired for political reasons

No one at work calls Julie
a Communist anymore.

HIGHER IDEALS

Julie and I find a place of our own,
a one-room, slightly furnished flat.

I have no talent for baking cookies,
         just like my mother.
I have no patience
to put things in their place,
         just like my mother.
I have no interest in cleansers,
pails, and mops,
         just like my mother.

Dust collects in every corner,
and Julie, sweet man, jokes about it.
"We have higher ideals," he says.

Ethel and Julius as a young married
couple enjoying time at a park, 1942

AT THE PARK

Julie wraps an arm around me
and pulls me into him.

Julie wraps his arm around me
like the holder around a Sabbath candle.

Julie wraps his arm around me,
my skin singes against his chest.

I was a closed shell in the sand,
now newly opened. I didn't know

I could smile offstage
until I met Julius.

THE EAST SIDE CONFERENCE TO DEFEND AMERICA AND CRUSH HITLER
JUNE 1941

Hitler betrays Stalin and invades the Soviet Union.
The Soviet Union stands alone.

The Communist Party of America calls for us
to get the United States into the war.

The Party forms committees so Americans can help
the Soviet Union face Nazi Germany on its own.

I want to help! I march into the office
of one of the committees, the East Side Conference.

Hail to my new boss who accepts me
as a full-time voluntary secretary.

Hail to the 7,000 who march throughout the Lower East Side
in a Parade of Nations to show solidarity.

Hail to the 100,000 spectators,
cheering the anti-Nazi rally.

Hail to my sweetheart, Julius, who has no objection
to my working for victory against the Nazis round the clock.

A DECEMBER UNLIKE ANY OTHER
DECEMBER 7, 1941

A Japanese attack surprises
the American fleet at Pearl Harbor in Hawaii
and the rest of us
who wake up to the news.

A Japanese bomb weighing nearly two tons
crashes onto the USS *Arizona*
and sinks it and its thousand sailors.

A Japanese torpedo rips open
the USS *Oklahoma*,
sending it to the depths of the Pacific.

Dozens of tortured battleships, cruisers, destroyers,
hundreds of destroyed airplanes.

Japan has made its move against America,
wanting to expand its territory
wanting our oils, minerals
wanting to behave like its allies, Germany and Italy.

December 8
Congress approves
Roosevelt's
declaration of war
against Japan.

December 11
Germany and Italy
declare war on America.
The Three Pigs Pact requires it.
We declare war
on Germany and Italy.

The Communist Party's *Daily Worker*
might be relieved that now
America will support the Soviet Union's
fight against Germany,
But I toss and turn at night,
wondering selfishly
what America going to war will mean
for Julie
for Bernie
for Dovey.

MISSION TO MOSCOW

My boss at the Conference
has been drafted
and before he leaves,
he gives me a copy
of *Mission to Moscow*,
written by a former U.S.
ambassador to the Soviet Union.

The book says Communism is no different
than working for the brotherhood of all men.

That's all Julie and I want.

PART II | KNICKERBOCKER VILLAGE

THREE ROOMS WITH A VIEW
APRIL 1942

Julie gets a promotion
and he buys me, of all things,
a fur coat! Now we can move
out of this one-room apartment.

We find a new apartment, back in Manhattan
on the Lower East Side, in a housing project.
At least now we'll have a bedroom,
bathroom, and kitchen.

We sign a two-year lease
on the eleventh floor
with a view of the courtyard.

BERNIE ENLISTS

MAY 1942

My brother Bernie has enlisted
in the U.S. Army.

Now he's going to be trained
to fire a gun
and kill people.

I tuck a photo of him
in his new military uniform
into the corner of my
bedroom dresser mirror.

His wife, Gladdy, will not be the only one
who will miss him
and pray that he'll come back
when the war's over
in tip-top shape.

I should have ripped up
his draft card two years ago.

THE HEROES' HOUR
SEPTEMBER 1942

Time to celebrate the worker
and war heroes at a huge Labor Day
rally in Central Park.
There's New York City Mayor La Guardia
There's singer Paul Robeson
There's a female Russian sniper
　　　　　because we're fighting alongside the Soviets
Hail to the Americans—
　　　　　Merchant marines
　　　　　Army nurses
　　　　　The Navy
　　　　　The Marine Corps
　　　　　The Coast Guard
All unify to "Smash Hitler."
Some man I've never seen before
catches Julie
in conversation. Once we're back
home, Julie says, "I want to work
with the Russians."

JULIE WANTS TO HELP

He makes lists of all his engineering friends.
He makes calls.
He visits them.
He comes home with papers.
He compiles documents, drawings, specifications.
He organizes them into folders.
He takes them to this Russian man with a code name.

Maybe they can help the Soviets against Hitler.
It is just as I imagined.

LIGHTING THE CANDLE AT BOTH ENDS

By day, an engineer
By night, a recruiter.

By day, a government worker
By night, helping the Soviet cause.

By day, my caring, tender man
hates to see people in pain.

By night, my caring, tender man
holds me tight in his arms.

DOVEY GOOFS OFF

Dovey, straighten up.
You're so busy with Ruthie
that you flunked all your college courses.
What good then was the reference
Julius gave you to get into engineering school?

So now the school has kicked you out.
You married Ruthie.
You're
only twenty-one.
What do you really know of life?

I only hope you can hold on to a job
and the furniture Mama and Papa gave you,
including my old bed.

THE ROSENBERG FAMILY EXPANDS

I so want to be a good mother;
I know what bad parenting looks like.

I expected this tiny being
Julie and I made

to make me bigger, but I didn't
expect the back pain.

Julie travels more than ever
and I am alone

patting my stomach
and talking to my womb.

IT'S A BOY!
MARCH 1943

The greatest gift a mother can bring
is a boy to the family.

The greatest gift a mother can bring
is joy to the family.

THE CIRCUMCISION CEREMONY

The rabbi rubs a little wine
on Michael Allen Rosenberg's
lips. The baby smacks them.

My papa is here. Julie's brother,
Dave, and his wife, too. We name
Dave and his wife Michael's
godparents. Dave is a pharmacist
and his wife a nurse.

Dovey and his new wife, Ruthie,
are also here.

But Julie is in Florida
on a work assignment,
and so the wine doesn't taste so sweet.

DOVEY'S OFF TO WAR
APRIL 1943

The draft has caught up with Dovey.
He's gone to Maryland for basic machine school.

He manages to come home one weekend,
and he and Ruthie join Julie and me

at the movies. Julie whispers
something to Dovey. I can't hear.

I add the photo of Dovey in uniform
to the dresser mirror.

THE GREAT MYSTERY

I wish I knew the secrets of caring for infants.
I wish I knew how to balance the demands
of a wife and the demands of a mother.

I can only be me and no one could
love this child more. I will spend
every moment of my life

letting this boy know how much
he is loved. No matter how loud
he cries, no matter how often.

I love you, I'll say
          as I play with his toes.
More than life, I'll say
          as I curl my fingers with his.
You are the world to me, I'll say,
          as I tickle his tummy,
his tiny fingers and wails reaching for me.

I find comfort with my brothers' wives. I've even
reached out to my mother. I bring
Michael to her Friday night dinner table.

Family is the wine we drink
to usher in the Sabbath.
The dinner is never peaceful.
We wish each other a peaceful week,
knowing full well that peace is out of our reach.

DOVEY GOES WEST

JUNE 1943

Dovey's stirring up trouble,
arguing with his superiors.

Dovey's transferred to Los Angeles
to work at a General Motors plant.

Dovey joins the 305th Ordnance Regiment,
Ordnance Base Machine Shop.

Dovey's transferred again to San Francisco
to inspect equipment before it's shipped overseas.

Dovey then moves to Pomona,
another ordnance base, to fix tank motors.

Ruthie tells me Dovey's making money on the side,
customizing small weapons for officers. Ruthie says, "You know,

he tested as a genius in his IQ tests."
That is most certainly a lie. I'm not as gullible as his wife.

RELATIVITY

Gladdy, Ruthie, and I attend Communist Party events.
We have a girls' night out
at the movies.
Ruthie
looks to me
for political guidance.
Despite her age,
she handles Dovey's absence well.
She is grand and I respect her opinions.
But it's too bad she's attached herself
to Mama's hip. No good will come of that.
Still, she dotes on Michael,
and he loves the stuffed animal she gave him.

ONE SONG TO SING
1944

I choose songs to show
there is still good in the world,
that despite the war
we could all live in peace.

I choose songs to show
that music is the universal language,
a song can lift us up when we're down.
The right song could stop the tanks and guns.

I want to choose one song to sing
to bring some to laughter, some to tears,
all to recognize nothing good comes from war.
But I don't know what song that would be.

BERNIE'S INJURED!

MAY 1944

My mother receives a telegram
from the War Office. She shrieks
even before opening it.

"You read it," she says.
Bernie's in the military hospital,
something about a tank accident,
his hand and face.

"He's alive, and he's going to stay alive,"
I say. "That's all there is to it."

DOVEY MOVES AGAIN

MAY 1944

Will he go overseas?
That's what Dovey thought.
Instead, his unit lands in Mississippi
for more machinist work.

A LETTER TO DOVEY

We want to hear from you. Mama
and Papa have made me their
designated scribe. So here I am,
your nephew nuzzling in my lap,
writing you in California from New York.
Ruthie and I went to see *Destination Tokyo*
in Times Square. It's about a submarine's
secret mission to gather intelligence
for an upcoming raid. I think you'd like it.

Movies help us take our minds
off worrying about you boys. Bernie's
been wounded in Europe—a tank accident.
He's in the hospital, something about
his face and hands, but he'll be all right
and back in action on the front lines. Don't
say anything to Papa about it. Now, will we
have to worry about you, too?

So, lazy boy, please write at least
once a week. It's been three weeks
without a word from you. Mama's
been frantic. Ruthie says all is A-okay,
but we want to hear from you. It really
is thoughtless and neglectful of you
to make us wait like this.

PARENTING

If I want to do something right,
I read.

If I want to do something right,
I seek out experts.

So why shouldn't I
devour parenting magazines
for the latest childrearing advice?

Why shouldn't I
go to the professionals and learn
how to be the best possible mother?

D-DAY!

JUNE 1944

"That the Yanks are coming,
the Yanks are coming,"

Allied troops storm the coast of occupied France.
Rat-a-tat-tat!
We'll show Hitler who's boss!

"We'll be over,
we're coming over,
and we won't come back till it's over
over there!"

DOVEY HAS A SECRET

JULY 1944

Julie and I take Dovey and Ruthie
out for paella.

"I'm finally going overseas,"
Dovey says. "But I don't think
I'll see combat."

Yet, according to Ruthie,
when Dovey goes back to Mississippi
after being with us in New York,
his unit is leaving for Europe without him.
Seems those in charge don't care for him.

Now he's transferred again to a different unit,
a special engineer detachment in the South somewhere.
He's excited, Ruthie says, because he's
in a government-run town, which suits
his Communist-leaning heart. Ruthie says
he's working on a classified project. Mum's
the word from now on.

CHARISMA

It's no wonder to me
that Julie is a successful recruiter.

He draws people to him
with an invisible, irretractable cord.

His clear arguments, the pure force
of his words persuade others to "join us."

He's brought Dovey and Ruthie
into his network of people to help the Soviet Union.

I prefer to stay out of it
I don't need a code name other than Mommy.

DOVEY'S BACK OUT WEST
AUGUST 1944

Still working on this secret project,
Dovey transfers to New Mexico. He
must be a machinist in demand.

What could be so secret among
the mesas of New Mexico?

A secret weapon to stop the war?
Dovey's in the thick of it now.
If only he could help stop this
dreadful destruction.

ALL IN THE FAMILY

OCTOBER 1944

It's settled
Julie has recruited Dovey into his circle
Julie has recruited Ruthie into his circle.

THE THREE AMIGOS
1945

We're three caballeros—
Gladdy, Ruthie, and I—
we squeezed into a recording booth
to sing a silly song
and press it on a 78 long-playing record,
sending it off to Bernie and Dovey.

These records are the new Victory mail,
V-mail we call it, to send
to U.S. soldiers. Bernie and Dovey
will be able to hear our voices
and our love.

RUTHIE SAYS GOODBYE

"I'm moving to Albuquerque,"
Ruthie says to me, "To join Dovey."

She's given up their New York
apartment. She'll find a new one

in New Mexico and a new job, too.
"Couldn't you just keep visiting?"

I ask. "It's a long trip," she says. "I'll
give the address to your mother."

We vow to write each other.
War is breaking apart our family.

JULIE LOSES HIS JOB
MARCH 1945

"Sweetheart," Julie says
as he comes through the door,
"I've been fired. It's illegal, I'm sure of it."

His snow-covered
hat and coat soak the sofa
while I hug his frustration tight.

Aren't the U.S. and U.S.S.R.
allies in the fight against
fascism?

Aren't we innocent
until proven guilty?
Since when has it been

a crime to believe
in the power of the people
and the elimination of poverty?

"I'm going to Washington," Julie says.
"Maybe our congressman can help.
I have to get my job back."

Julie goes to Washington.
Julie comes home,
disappointment stretched
across his face.

Still, I believe in his talent and he soon
finds work, as I knew he would—
with a promotion and a raise, no less—
doing Army/Navy research projects for a radio company.

RAISE THAT FLAG!

The newspapers are full of this photo
of five marines hoisting the American flag
on the Japanese island of Iwo Jima.
We aim to keep America for ourselves!
No Japanese takeover for us in the Pacific!

I don't believe in war and killing.
But the sight of these men and the flag
fills me with Stars-and-Stripes pride.

THE DEATH OF THE PRESIDENT
APRIL 1945

Roosevelt is dead!
A stroke killed him.
The whole city mourns.
The whole country mourns.
The whole world mourns.
I hold Michael tight and rock.

DING-DONG! THE EVIL HITLER'S DEAD

Hi, low, the bunker's cold
Hitler's gone to where goblins go—
Down below, below!
Hi, low, he's dealt himself his own death blow
Ding-dong, Hitler's gone, I'll sing it high, sing it low!

THE *LIFE* WE DIDN'T KNOW
MAY 1945

A small boy in a striped sweater and short pants
saunters down a lane
past a row of Jewish corpses
near the Bergen-Belsen
concentration camp in Germany.

A small boy doesn't know these people
were murdered because they were Jewish.
He looks away. He doesn't see their nakedness,
their emaciated bodies, their abandonment by the world.

Any one of these bodies could have been
my cousins. If my parents hadn't come
to America, these bodies could have been us.

Smoke still smolders from the chimneys
where other bodies were burned,
their ashes floating up to the sky.

Julie finds me mumbling Kaddish,
the Jewish mourner's prayer.

THE FOUR QUESTIONS
TWO MONTHS AFTER PASSOVER

Why does a government allow its people to live in poverty?
    Things are looking up.
Why can't we believe in what we want to believe in?
    We still read and distribute the *Daily Worker*, though not to
    so many people anymore.

Why must there be hate?
    We've seen what hate brings: death and destruction.
    There's hate because people are afraid.
Why must there be war?
    I still can't answer this.

A NEW TAKE ON "THE NUTCRACKER SUITE"
AUGUST 1945

A fairy dust sprinkled from above
brings dancing mushrooms to life
as they bow and nod to *The
Nutcracker Suite.*

But in reality, the cargo holds
of fighter planes drop
atom bomb fairy dust on two
Japanese cities.

The dancing mushrooms
grow
and grow
and grow
into monstrous gray clouds of death.

The only music, screams of the planes,
screams of the writhing, silence of the dead.

World War II is over, everywhere.

THE TRUTH ABOUT DOVEY AND NEW MEXICO
AUGUST 1945

Now that two Japanese cities
lay in atom bomb ruins

Now that the bombs' huge mushroom clouds
appear in newspaper and magazine photographs

Now that secrets explode about
atomic bomb development

in Los Alamos, New Mexico,
where Dovey was transferred last year.

What role did Dovey play?

JULIE LOSES HIS JOB—AGAIN

No more war
No more war effort
No more research needed—
Julie no longer needed.

THE BEGINNING OF A NEW WORLD ORDER

SEPTEMBER 1945

The United States
occupies South Korea.

                              The Soviet Union
                         occupies North Korea.

          Former friends, now enemies
             pitted against each other.

THE UN-AMERICANS
NOVEMBER 1945

An un-American—the former head of the Communist Party of
    America
An un-American—the Party's secretary
Un-Americans—Party leaders who ran for the U.S. Presidency
Un-Americans—75,000 members of the Party
So says this House Un-American Activities Committee
that's rounding up Party leaders into forced hearings.

G-d bless Un-America,
land that I love.

ALL BACK TOGETHER
MARCH 1946

Dovey and Ruthie are home for good,
and I'm glad. The family has been reunited.

Something changed in New Mexico. They don't
want to attend Communist meetings anymore.

Even when Julie mentions it, Ruthie leaves the room
and Dovey tries to change the subject.

"You can stay with us for a while if you need to,"
I say. Ruthie is pregnant. I could look after her

so she doesn't miscarry again. It must have been
hard for her to be alone most of the time in New Mexico.

BLOW OUT
MARCH 1946

Oak Ridge, Tennessee,
a major atom bomb manufacturing plant,

Oak Ridge, Tennessee,
the site of stolen secrets

by Americans duped by the Soviets.
The House Un-American Activities

and the FBI are on the hunt for a foreign spy ring
operating between New York and Oak Ridge.

Didn't Dovey work in Tennessee?
Has he been working on the bomb?

LET'S SING A NEW TUNE

What if the FBI and
the House Un-American Activities Committee
add New Mexico to the New York–Tennessee spy ring?
What if they bring in Dovey for questioning?
What if they interrogate Julie?
What then?
What songs will they sing?

If it were me, I'd sing,
"Let the Red, Red Robin
Go Bob-Bob-Bobbing Along."

A FRESH START
APRIL 1946

"Start your own
business," I say, "Be your own boss."

I get my brothers to help.
Bernie invests his money. Dovey, now discharged,

invests his machinist skills.
They should be able to make a go of it.

They name their enterprise, G & R Engineering,
for Greenglass and Rosenberg.

A NEW MAIN EVENT

During the war, the Soviets were our friends.
After the war, the Soviets are our enemies.
Superpowers in the boxing ring,
expected to duke out this Cold War with
nuclear bomb threats stuffed
in their boxing gloves.

In this corner, America, leader of the Free World and democracy.
In the opposite corner, the Soviet Union and Communism.

A dark fear against anything and anyone Communist
slithers across the canvas floor.
Everything we stood for before and during the war
makes Julie and me un-American.

TOUGH BUSINESS

G & R isn't faring well,
and an investor pulls out.
Bernie tries to keep the peace

between Dovey and Julie,
who constantly bicker.
We're strapped for cash.

I don't mind for myself.
I can deal with wearing
the same clothes.

At the grocer's the other
day, I realized I hadn't
the cash for our dinner.

I heard Mama say
so many times during
the lean times,

"Could you please extend
me credit? I have children's
mouths to feed."

Now I say the same thing.
It's amazing how many
meals can come

from one roast chicken.

HOW DARE SHE?

On my way back home from running
an errand, another mother
sneers at me. Sneers!
She says, "You Jewish mothers.
You let your kids do whatever they want."

I am not a violent person, but I want
to assault her with cutting words—or a bat.
"At least I don't keep my child on a leash!" I want to say.
"At least my child is clean!" I want to say.
"Who the heck are you to judge?" I want to say.

I am certainly not the only Jewish woman
in Knickerbocker Village. And what if
I pay attention to what the experts
say about not restricting
our children, to allow them
to express themselves?

My little Michael has more brains
in his head at four than most adults.
So there.

"HOW TO SPOT A COMMUNIST"

I am flipping magazine pages at the corner newsstand,
where I usually pick up my copies of *Parents' Magazine*,
when I spot the new issue of *Look* magazine, March 4, 1947.

Check before you sign that petition.
Check before you join that club.
You could be supporting the Communist cause.

Communists wear black.
Americans wear white.

Possible Communists:
>Neighbor
>Union leader
>Organization

Characteristics:
>Aggressive
>Frustrated
>Deprived
>Weak
>Kvetchy (my word)

Failure to recognize a Communist
will make America weak.
So they say in one of the country's most popular magazines.

BIRTHS

MAY 1947

The G & R Engineering Company
folds. In its place,
the birth of the new Pitt Machine Company.

Julius Rosenberg, President.
Dovey Greenglass, Vice President.
Bernie Greenglass, Secretary.

I give birth, too, to another
beautiful boy, Robert. We
call him Robby, because

such a formal name does not
suit his sweet face, the cheeks
I just want to pinch.

He looks like me, and Michael
looks like Julie. Who can ask
for more than that?

WILL THE REAL KOREA PLEASE STAND UP?
1948

South Korea,
now on its own,
elects a new leader,
American style.

North Korea,
now on its own,
has its own version
of Stalin.

Both say they're the legitimate Korea.
They can't both be right.

REQUIEM FOR MY DEAR PAPA
MARCH 1949

Sewing machine oil in all
your creases, you spent years
hunched over obligations,

the weight of Mama forcing
your body and backbone to the ground.
What were your dreams

when you left Russia for America?
Now buried in Queens waiting for Mama,

your oiled skin
merges with flesh dust
and you return home.

THANK YOU, DEAR HUSBAND

My sweet Julie,
how kind it is of you to pay for
Papa's funeral. We have been married
for nearly ten years. It is impossible
for me to think about my life
before you. It is impossible
for me to exist without you.

TESTING, TESTING
AUGUST 1949

The Soviet Union has just
made its first test
of the atom bomb.

Testing, testing,
Americans grow more scared
than ever before.

All throughout the neighborhood,
people are asking: What will
the Russians do with the bomb?

The schools have posted
big yellow signs pointing toward
their basements: Fallout Shelter.

RED AND WHITE

1950

Democracy

                                                    Communism

                        cut America
                and divide the world.

THIS IS YOUR FBI

The Equitable Life Insurance Society
of the United States presents
This Is Your FBI,
the official broadcast from the files
of the Federal Bureau of Investigation.
Tonight's FBI file: "Yesterday's Killers."

I'm putting the dinner plates away,
and Michael settles in for his favorite
radio show. In fourteen minutes,
an Equitable representative will talk about
how this is a good time for parents to plan
ahead for their children.

I think I can get everything put away in time.
I listen to how J. Edgar Hoover and his G-Men
attacked gangster crime in the 1930s. I remember.

JULIE GETS UNEASY

"I wonder if Dovey knew this scientist
Klaus Fuchs in New Mexico?" Julie asks
as he dries the dishes.

"Why do you ask?"

"Fuchs was arrested in London
for being a Soviet spy. The papers
say he gave the Soviets plans
for the hydrogen bomb,
for the atom bomb—"

"Is Dovey in trouble?
Are you in trouble?"

"No, we've got nothing to worry about."
He puts the dishes in the wrong cabinet.

WHO WILL WIN THE BOMB RACE?

America showed the power of the bomb in Japan.
Most of America is scared of the Soviet Union.
They mistakenly believe
that in the Soviet Union, there is:

      No freedom of thought

      No freedom of speech

      No freedom to buy what you want

      No freedom of where to live

      No freedom of where to work.

All eyes are on American bomb secrets
that could now be in the hands of Soviet scientists.

J. EDGAR HOOVER SEEKS AND PROMISES TO FIND

We have to search for the Communists, Hoover says.
We have to find Klaus Fuchs's messenger, he says,
and then a while later, he and his FBI men find him.

I imagine Hoover as a vacuum cleaner,
snaking along the floor
looking for anything that resembles a speck of dirt.

When I see photos of him in the papers,
I hear the sucking of the vacuum hose
hunting, hunting, hunting until it swallows anyone who gets in
    his way.

THE PAPERS SAY

It could be next year, the papers say,
when the Soviet Union could
wipe out the United States, Canada,
Britain, the Netherlands, France,
Belgium, and others with the bomb.

The papers say,
the Soviets pose a real threat.

The papers say,
we should watch our harbors.

The papers say, Fuchs's messenger
is a chemist from Philadelphia.
He passed Fuchs's information
to his Soviet contacts.

The papers say,
more names and more arrests are coming.
The papers say the chemist wanted
to help the Soviet Union,
an ally in the war,
win against Nazi Germany.

The papers say, the FBI now looks
for a machinist who worked on the bomb.
A machinist who worked in New Mexico.
The machinist who gave the Soviets our secrets.

Before the papers can say,
I already know in my heart:
It's Dovey.

SENATOR JOE MCCARTHY IS AN UGLY MAN

An ugly man is one who casts aspersions.
An ugly man is one who was elected to office
but has his own agenda.
An ugly man accuses everyday citizens.
An ugly man writes a letter to President Truman,
accusing 57 men in the State Department
of being card-carrying Communists.
This ugly man insists a spy ring
operates in the State Department.
This ugly man says the State Department
is riddled with Reds.
An ugly man is new senator Joseph R. McCarthy.

MCCARTHY FANS THE FLAMES OF THE "RED SCARE"

Does this man know no bounds?
McCarthy now accuses employees
in the White House
in the Treasury Department
in the U.S. Army
of being Reds.

I'll bet he's made sure
his wife no longer wears
red lipstick and has removed
all shades of red
from his daughter's Crayola box.

DEADLY DOMINOES

JUNE 1950

North Korea
invades South Korea.
The Soviet Union
supports North Korea.
The United States
supports South Korea.
The Cold War
is global, real, and deadly.
Which domino will fall
toward Communism?
Which domino will tip
toward democracy?
At home and abroad,
we all gallop
toward an apocalypse.

WE'RE BEING WATCHED

"We're being watched,"
Julie says one night
as I wash the dishes
and he dries. Michael
listens to the radio
and little bunny Robby
is already in slumberland
in the bedroom.
(Julie and I sleep in
the living room.)

I'm not naïve, really, I'm not,
but how could helping
the Soviet Union
defeat Hitler
make us the bad guys?

My brother has done nothing wrong
as far as I know. Except that he's not all that bright.
We have done nothing wrong
as far as I know.

VISITORS

JUNE 1950

As I'm washing the breakfast
dishes, scraping remains
of stubborn oatmeal
from a bowl, Julie
goes to the bathroom
to shave.

A stern knock at the door,
it's only 8:00 a.m.,
brings Julie out in his
undershirt.

"Open up, this is the FBI,"
a voice says. The agents
allow Julie to finish his shave
and put on a shirt. They
are taking him to the federal
building at Foley Square.

Hours later, Julie comes home, weary.
He says, "They asked me all sorts
of questions about Dovey:
His education
His work
When did he come home on furlough.

And, here's the worst of it,
they said
I told Dovey to give information
to the Soviets."

My head swirls. Julie announces,
"I need a lawyer."

SAY NOTHING

Tonight, Julie doesn't say much to me,
just that according to the newspaper,
Dovey has been arraigned
and held on $100,000 bond. Julie
says the charges
against himself are crazy.

Julie goes out to meet
with a defense lawyer, someone
recommended by the engineers' union
lawyers. He's Manny Bloch,
who has built a clientele of
Soviet sympathizers.

Julie comes home and asks
about the boys. He kisses me.
"If anything happens," Julie says,
"we have to be prepared. We must
say nothing. We must be strong.
This is Manny Bloch's counsel."

Manny says, "Show no fear."
I am afraid for Julie.
I am afraid for our sweet boys.
I am afraid, yes, for myself.

I AM THE LONE RANGER

A month later Julie reads the evening paper,
Michael listens to *The Lone Ranger*
on the radio.
Seven FBI agents burst in,
two seize Julie's arms,
the remaining five raid
the apartment like flames.

"I want a lawyer," I scream.
Michael hugs my leg and I hear
Robby's cry from the bedroom,
and now Michael's got my other leg.
The agents open all drawers and cabinets,
confiscate my typewriter, photos,
letters, bills, birth certificates,
whatever paper they can lay their
hands on, even my *Parents' Magazine*.

"This is a violation of our rights," I
yell. "You need a warrant."
The FBI push the boys and me into the bedroom.
When we're allowed back into the living room,
my beloved is gone.
I didn't even get to kiss him goodbye.

THE AFTERMATH

It's 9:00 p.m. "Would you be
comfortable somewhere else?"
these smug men in their suits
ask. All I can think of is
64 Sheriff Street.

As we stuff into the FBI's black sedan,
Michael asks, "Will Daddy be home tonight?"
"No," I say, "not tonight."

SUMMER LAMENT

I am alone on this summer night,
Our home ravaged, our family torn,
My husband in handcuffs, wrists held tight.

Drivers honk horns with all their might.
They do not know upstairs I mourn.
I am alone on this summer night.

A black car parks, turns off its headlights.
Dark shadows inside, mirrors of scorn.
My husband in handcuffs, wrists held tight.

I toss and turn, I don't know what's right.
Accused of treason! Enemy sworn!
I am alone on this summer night.

My heart is breaking, future's not bright.
My screams, my yells, my boys now forlorn.
My husband in handcuffs, wrists held tight.

And you, my love, cell walls your sole sight.
Embrace me, love me, until the morn.
I am alone on this summer night.
Dear one, you in handcuffs, wrists held tight.

THEY SAY

We are Communists
Julius is a spy
Passing vital secrets to the Soviets
Compromising American democracy
Betraying all Americans
Committing
      Treason
      Conspiracy
      Espionage.

The Feds are crazy.

THE DAY AFTER'S PRESS CONFERENCE

Attention, please!
I, Mrs. Julius Rosenberg,
call you reporters to order.

I stand in my galley kitchen
in a sundress and sandals,
the perfect portrait

of Julius's little wife.
I pose for cameras,
making sure my wedding ring

is visible. I dry dishes. I make
no effort to hide the rusting,
peeling enamel trash pail.

Neither my husband nor I
have ever been Communists.
This whole thing is ridiculous.

(I am doing exactly what Julie
and I have talked about.
Deny everything.
Show no fear.)

We're having chicken for dinner.

Ethel washes dishes while holding a
press conference in her apartment the
day after Julius's arrest, July 1950.

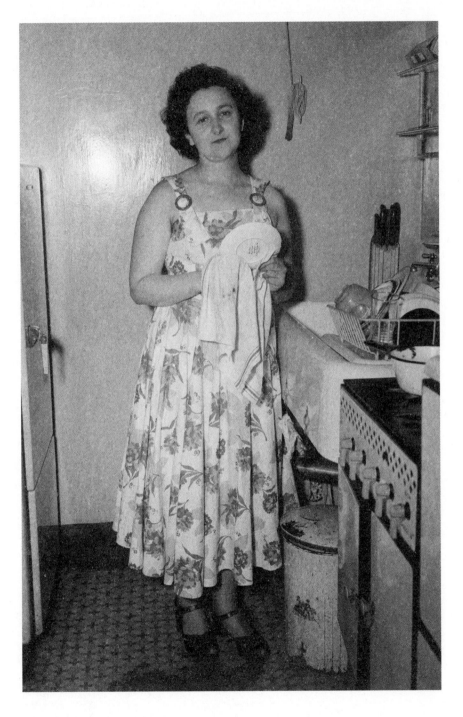

I SEE IT IN THE PHOTO

You appear on page 1 of the *New York Times*.
The article says you're the fourth

spy picked up for espionage—
giving atomic secrets to the Soviets.

I get to page 8 in the *Daily News*.
The portrait shows my mournful eyes.

This is all still surreal.
Your boys never stop asking for you:

"When is Daddy coming home?"
"Can't I call Daddy on the phone?"

"Tell Daddy how much I miss him!"
"Don't forget to tell him!"

A TYPICAL SPY

Doesn't attend Communist Party meetings
Doesn't read Communist newspapers
Doesn't engage in conversations about
      the Soviet Union
      Communism.

A typical spy stays behind the scenes,
is a loner.

Julie is upfront.
Julie does not hide.
Julie is not a typical spy.

DEAR JULIE

I don't mean to cry
during our short visits.

I don't mean to ignore
your questions.

But I don't want to talk
about your business

and who to contact about this or that.
I want to talk about us,

our boys, how lonely I
am for you.

While the boys sleep,
I pull your pillow toward me

Pretending it's you
Pretending I hear your breathing

Pretending I play with your whiskers
Pretending your warmth rubs my temples

Pretending your empty space is only a nightmare.
"I will straighten out this trouble," you write.

I know you will make everything all right.

MY FIRST GRAND JURY HEARING
AUGUST 1950

The assistant federal prosecutor asks:
Who were the members of your husband's spy ring?
I refuse to answer on the grounds that it may incriminate me.

Did you sign a Communist Party candidate petition?
Yes, I did.

Then I stick to Manny Bloch's advice, no matter what I'm asked:
I refuse to answer
I refuse to answer
I refuse to answer.

Only afterward do I realize
how big this is. A federal grand jury.
How long will pleading the Fifth Amendment satisfy?
I hope Mr. Bloch's got more in his legal arsenal than this.

CAT AND MOUSE

I rush from the federal building
to pick up Michael and Robby
at my mother's.

I hear voices in the kitchen.
I make my way there
and both my mother and Ruthie stop talking.

I try to be polite. I say to Ruthie
what a good baby she has.
Ruthie turns red. She's incensed
about something. Me? She doesn't say.

There's a look about her,
like she's a cat who's
just caught and swallowed a mouse.

What does she know that I don't?

I spoiled their fun
by showing up. Now
they can't gossip about me.

I ask, "Were the boys any trouble?"
Mama bangs her hand on the table.
She shrills, "If you don't talk, you're
gonna burn with your husband."

A BETTER PLACE
AUGUST 1950

Mama's is no place for my boys
while I rush around the city
taking care of everything. I

contact the Jewish Community Homemakers Service
and make an appointment to place
Michael and Robby in a home,
only temporarily. My focus has to be
on Julie's release.

I admit I'm distracted,
because the Feds want to see me
again, Friday, August 11. One
appearance before the grand jury
wasn't enough for them.
I'm just going to say, "I refuse to answer,"
and run to the subway for my appointment
with the Homemakers Service.

BY THE SUBWAY STATION

After the assistant federal prosecutor asks me
the same questions I faced in the first hearing

After I scurry out of the courtroom
eager to make my appointment

After I reach the banister
and the stairs heading down to the subway

An arm reaches out and grips mine.
Two FBI agents corner me.

They say I have to come with them.
I am under arrest for espionage against the United States.

I NEED A LAWYER

I am allowed to phone Julie's lawyer,
but Manny Bloch is on vacation.
Instead I talk to his father, Alexander,
and he promises to come at once.

I've been in custody for about three hours
when I'm taken to meet
with the senior Mr. Bloch, a lovely man
in his seventies, but sadly not the kind of lawyer
with experience in espionage cases. I don't know
anyone else who can help.

The assistant prosecutor
charges me:
Conspiracy to commit espionage.
Together with my husband I plotted and spied
to give atomic bomb details to the Communists.
He wants to set bail at $100,000.
The senior Mr. Bloch argues the charges are flimsy
and explains that I'm a mother
of two small boys.
The prosecutor prevails
and the bail is set.

The world has turned upside down!
Surely I will wake up and find myself
back in my kitchen.

MY LAST PHONE CALL

"You can't come home?" Michael asks.

"No."

He screams.

> I hear that scream pass through my heart and into my blood.
> It will never leave me.

A LETTER FROM JULIE
ABOUT MY ARREST

"I heard the news over the radio . . .
I've been given permission to write . . .
How are you feeling . . .
How are the children?
Has any provision been made for them?
Are you keeping a stiff upper lip?"

I WRITE JULIE FROM THE WOMEN'S HOUSE OF DETENTION, GREENWICH VILLAGE

I am not cool, calm, or collected.
I will not be seeing you on Sunday.
I will not be making chicken for dinner.

SOME WORDS ABOUT THE CHARGES

In a world that could not have imagined
World War II, a federal law was put in place
to protect America in time of war
against foreign spies. Manny Bloch says
anyone convicted of giving a foreign government
information that compromises
America's national defense (even if an ally)
commits treason under
the Espionage Act of 1917,
could be put in prison for life
or get the death sentence.

The vital point:
What was right during the war
is now wrong.

Except we've done nothing wrong.

I wish I could lose myself in Julie's arms
and forget any of this madness is happening.

EACH NIGHT I ACHE

Allowed to write letters just once a month,
Each night I talk to you as if you were here.
We chat about the boys and how they're getting strong.
Spiritual songs lift me out of my blues.

Each night I talk to you as if you were here.
Planning for our future, the four of us,
Spiritual songs lift me out of my blues.
It is the only activity I look forward to.

Planning for our future, the four of us.
That's what's in my head during recreation hour.
It is the only activity I look forward to
Until I see you in court, when we face the jury together.

That's what's in my head during recreation hour.
The grand jury questions all our friends.
Until I see you in court
I don't know what to believe.

The grand jury questions all our friends.
Dovey and Ruth, who knows what garbage they're saying.
I don't know what to believe.
Manny Bloch says: Courage, confidence, persistence.

Dovey and Ruth, who knows what garbage they're saying.
I don't want to get Julie's friends in trouble.
Manny Bloch says: Courage, confidence, persistence.
It's all about naming names.

I don't want to get anyone in trouble.

Allowed to write letters just once a month.

It's all about naming names.

The only names important to me are Julius, Michael, and Robby.

WHAT TO DO WITH THE BOYS

Mama doesn't want them
    They're hard to discipline, she says.
    They're expensive to feed, she says.
One of Julie's sisters could take them
    But her husband thinks it's bad for his business.

We are pariahs.
We are the parents
of the most adorable little boys.
    What have I done?
    What must I do?
    How can I get us all back to where we were,
    snug and cozy in Knickerbocker Village?

Right now we have no choice:
Hebrew Children's Home in the Bronx.

THE NEW ATHLETIC STAR OF THE WOMEN'S DETENTION CENTER

Prostitutes
Drug dealers
Embezzlers
are kinder to me
than the women of
Knickerbocker Village.

We play catch on the rooftop.
We play softball.
I hit three home runs.
I like the way it feels to smash a ball,
feel the wind and the sun.

But none of it compares
to receiving a letter
from Michael in his own handwriting.

MAMA VISITS

It goes something like this:

"Behave more like Dovey and Ruth!"

> You mean, lie.

"Give the government what it wants!"

> You mean, lie.

"Save Dovey, save yourself!"

> You mean, lie.

"You dirty Communist!"
"Divorce Julius!"

> "Enough!
> Don't come here anymore."

> Dearest Julie, we must think
> about foster care for our boys.

> I think we'll agree: A family is much better
> than an orphanage.

PART III | FEDERAL COURTHOUSE, FOLEY SQUARE

THE TRIAL DATE IS SET

It is unsettling to read about oneself
in the pages of *The New York Times*.
The paper says atomic bomb project leader
Robert Oppenheimer will testify against us.

The date is set:
March 6, 1951.

Ethel and Julius in the van that escorts
them to their March 1951 trial

OPENING DAY
MARCH 6, 1951

"You're going to wear that?" my new friends at the jail ask.
I don't care about the photographers, how
the jury sees me. I only know I'm going to see
Julie, and it's his opinion that matters.

I wear a white blouse, dark skirt,
and a wide-brimmed hat. My friends offer
me a scarlet blouse, but that reminds
me of blood and guilt.

We are innocent. White is purity.

When I enter the wood-paneled courtroom,
it is already filled with reporters
and curious spectators. It is like walking
into the mouths of lions, readying jaws and paws for the kill.
I take my seat at the defense table
next to Julie.

Julie and I have put all our faith in Manny Bloch
and his father. I pray they have the experience
to pull this off. Despite the papers, the radio,
J. Edgar Hoover and his FBI, we have done nothing wrong.

The prosecutor speaks first and reels off a list
of more than 100 witnesses he intends to call.
He accuses us of treason and Communism.
The crowd seems to agree. I know that all eyes

have been on North Korea lately,
and the fight between the United States
and the Soviet Union. But here, in this courtroom,
the lives of two Americans hang in the balance.

MY LITTLE BROTHER IN A NEW LIGHT

The only true statement Dovey makes
is his legal name, David Greenglass.
He's far more imaginative than
Julie or I ever gave him credit for.
He conjures up meetings and conversations
that never happened.
He makes up a story
about a Jell-O box side panel that Julie
ripped off, that he tore in half,
gave one half to Ruthie so she'd
recognize the messenger spy.
Dovey makes up another story,
that I typed up his notes
about atomic bombs.

We know Dovey is cooperating with
the FBI to protect himself. It takes
all my discipline to appear
unmoved.

SURELY, RUTHIE WILL TELL THE TRUTH

It goes something like this:

"I was too young to realize fully the thing at the time."
"I was always under the impression
that Julius lost his job
because Ethel
was a card-carrying Communist."
"Julius knew David was working on the atomic bomb."

Lies, lies, lies.

PEEK-A-BOO, I SEE YOU

Jell-O is a slimy, shaky, see-through dessert.
Jell-O is a flavored powder mixed with boiling water.
Jell-O comes in a palm-size box.
Ruthie says I served Jell-O one night at our apartment.
Ruthie says Julie tore the side of the box in half
      Half for her so the Soviet messenger could identify her
         in Albuquerque
      Half for Julie to keep to give to the Soviet messenger
      They'd match up their pieces.
I never served Jell-O, especially not red raspberry.
We're more of a chocolate pudding family,
we Rosenbergs.

SMOKE AND MIRRORS

There are no 100 witnesses,
no celebrity scientists,
to testify against us.
But the prosecution calls
Ruthie's messenger, Harry Gold—
who'd worked with Klaus Fuchs—
spy Elizabeth Bentley,
Julie's City College classmates.
The prosecution wants to pressure us
into some confession
that is not ours to give.
But it is mostly brother against sister,
family against family. And Dovey
holds the smoking gun.

What are my boys doing right now?

JULIUS ON THE WITNESS STAND

He's lost weight.
He sits, his back against
the chair, legs crossed,
hands in his lap. He looks
handsome, though gaunt,
in his gray suit, white shirt,
and silver-and-maroon tie.

He refutes every claim made against him
over the course of three days. When
he finishes, he is spent. I want to cradle
him in my arms but cannot.

MY TURN AT BAT, NEARLY THREE WEEKS INTO THE TRIAL

It goes something like this:

I answer all my lawyer's questions:
    About marriage
    About children
    About the monthly rent
    About a table bought for $21 from Macy's.

But when the prosecutor wants to trap me:
"Did you help your brother join the Communist Party?"
I refuse to answer on the grounds
that it may incriminate me.
Manny Bloch objects to the line
of the prosecutor's questioning.
He moves for a mistrial
based on the flagrant prejudices,
based on the flimsy evidence
the prosecution presented.
Motion denied.

I refuse to answer
I refuse
I refuse.

JUDGE KAUFMAN'S INSTRUCTIONS TO THE JURY

You will consider whether the Rosenbergs
conspired to commit
an act of espionage to assist a foreign power.
As a reminder, a foreign power does not
necessarily mean an enemy power.

Consider the atomic bomb and other classified
information passed to assist a foreign government.

God bless you all.

THE JURY RETURNS ITS VERDICT

Eleven men and one woman deliberate, we're guilty.
They debate, seven hours and 42 minutes, guilty.

One of the jury found minimal evidence against me.
The judge required them to think again, both Rosenbergs, guilty.

It is all a set-up, a collusion with the FBI.
There was never a chance for a verdict other than guilty.

Judge, prosecutors, witnesses, the press—all see eye to eye.
My brother deceived them to convince the jury we're guilty.

Dovey plea-bargained protection, created mountainous lies.
Without eye contact, without remorse, he sealed our fate, guilty.

And, I, Ethel—the sister who held him and sang lullabies—
The faithful sister, who committed no crime, am now guilty.

MR. MANNY BLOCH SPEAKS TO THE PRESS

The Rosenbergs will appeal to the highest courts
of this land, and they will always maintain their
innocence. I think
Julius and Ethel Rosenberg
thought that in this political climate
it was almost impossible to overcome
a charge of this kind.

JUDGE KAUFMAN AND PROSECUTOR SAYPOL ADDRESS THE JURY

Your verdict is a correct verdict,
but this is a sad day for America.
I wish to thank J. Edgar Hoover
and the FBI and their cooperation
in this case
and the defense attorneys . . .

This trial was full, fair, and open.
Every opportunity was given to the defense
to present their case.

This case has ramifications so wide
that they involve the very question
of whether or when the devastation
of an atomic war may fall upon the world.

WE LEAVE THE COURTHOUSE

Julie is handcuffed and led out to his transport.
I am not handcuffed,
and I am returned to the Women's House of Detention.
I have a new cell on a different floor,
a new cell that directly faces the guard station.

Prison guards don't know me.
I will not try to commit suicide.
I am more determined than ever.
I will not show weakness.

When I attend Friday night Shabbat services,
more women attend than usual.
They are there to see me, to watch me crumble
under the weight of my verdict.
I will not succumb and I walk down
the aisle with measure and purpose in my step.

It is the Sabbath
and I am the Sabbath Queen.

SENTENCING

Julie is already in the prison van when it pulls up
to the Women's House of Detention. I sit
as close to him as the mesh screen allows. I
poke my fingers through the hold and place
them on his arrested hands.

The courtroom is standing room only
when we enter. We are summoned
to the bench and someone
places chairs there for us.

The prosecutor and Manny Bloch make their statements.
Manny admits to his inexperience, not the
best strategy.

At noon, the judge speaks at the same time
the bells of a nearby church peal,
as if what he's about to render comes
from divine providence.

He calls the act we've been convicted of
a crime worse than murder. He blames us
for the Korean War
for the loss of 50,000 American lives.

He says, Julie was at the helm of conspiracy. Then he
comes to me:
Ethel is a "full-fledged partner in this crime."
She should have deterred him from his "ignoble cause."

He says, cruelly, we placed our devotion to our cause
above our own personal safety,
that we were conscious of sacrificing our own children.
He sentences us
to death,
execution by electric chair
at Sing Sing prison, the week of May 21.

Julie turns to me and nods.

IT'S OVER

Four U.S. marshals surround me and Julie.
They escort us out a side door to holding cells
in the basement.
Julie is silent.
The marshals then usher us into a conference room.
I pass Manny Bloch's father, in tears. I hug him.
I say, "You did everything you could."
Julie takes a seat at the head of the table.
He tells the Blochs that
nothing they could have done
would have changed the outcome.
He says, "We will fight this, because we are innocent."

I hear later that Dovey receives fifteen years
in exchange for his betrayal of us.
I hear later that my mother sobs when she hears my sentence.

I am too numb to feel anything.
We are brought to the holding cells now.
Julie yells out to me, "Don't worry. Everything will be
all right. We are innocent." He expects public outrage to turn the tide.

I open my mouth, and a Puccini opera comes out.

THE SOUNDTRACK OF MY LIFE

I could imagine Puccini writing the soundtrack
of my life. I'd be wearing Madame Butterfly's
kimono, my face painted in white
with red rosebud lips. That one aria
she sings when the ship is in the harbor,
the one that rips your heart open
as the reeds weave into the chords.

I could imagine Mozart's flutes and violins
guiding my extreme highs and lows
like the Queen of the Night, spewing
staccato bullets
with my long, open mouth.

But if I could commission a composer,
I'd reach out to Romberg and his operettas,
light and fun. I need those operatic
sweethearts of the movies, that
Nelson Eddy march, Jeanette MacDonald
on his strong arm. The pacing,
staccato and determined. Arms swinging,
voices singing. One-two-three-four.
Stout-hearted Ethel Rosenberg
is on the march for freedom!

APPEALS

It may be futile,
but we have to try. They want
to pin the whole Korean War on us.
That without plans for the bomb
in Soviet hands, there'd be no Korean War,
no loss of American lives for no reason.

It may be futile,
but we have to try until they listen to reason.

ETHEL'S BLUES

Eight months without my boys, my arms a nest for no one.
No snuggles or sniffles, no sleep-time song in the night
Not a single giggle, no "Mommy" allowed, my sons.

No phone calls, no visits, Manny Bloch says it can't be done.
I sit here alone in my cave of cries, my jaw tight
Eight months without you boys, my arms a nest for no one.

I get your letters with fat crayoned lines, flaps undone.
Sometimes in stillness, I hear you, your squeals of delight
Not a single giggle, no "Mommy" allowed, my sons.

No wet kisses, no stubby fingers, no silly puns.
No water to quench dry mouths, no poetry to cite
Eight months without my boys, my arms a nest for no one.

Until we prove our innocence, when our case gets won,
We have to do without each other, endure the fight
Not a single giggle, no "Mommy" allowed, my sons.

Sweet Michael, dearest Robby, one day we will unite.
Your daddy reminds us, he'll make everything all right.
Eight months without my boys, my arms a nest for no one.
Give a single giggle, I am your Mommy, my sons.

PART IV | SING SING FEDERAL PRISON, OSSINING, NEW YORK

ARRIVAL

APRIL 11, 1951

They rush me out of the Women's House of Detention
      to Sing Sing.
All of a sudden, I can't tell Manny Bloch I'm en route
      to Sing Sing.

A sedan delivers me just before two o'clock
      to Sing Sing.
Sandwiched between two U.S. marshals, I climb the stairs
      to Sing Sing.

Press stand outside the fortress doors, their cameras ready
      at Sing Sing.
Their flashbulbs explode in front of my face, blinding me
      at Sing Sing.

No time for goodbyes to friends, inmates, before the trip
      to Sing Sing.
The law says I must be separated, that's why I'm here,
      Sing Sing.

The goal is clear, to get me quickly without fanfare
      to Sing Sing.
Taking me, breaking me might get Julie to talk
      at Sing Sing.

And I, Ethel, may never leave this place, my new home now
      Sing Sing.
I shelve books, hang up greeting cards in my Condemned Cell (CC)
      at Sing Sing.

MY NEW ABODE IN THE CCs

Birthday card from Julie,
cardboard picture frames I made
to hold photos of Michael and Robby.

Whenever I feel the urge
to let out my tortured screams,
to accept this bottomless horror,
I will look at these keepsakes
and bury my tears in another place and time.

LET MY PEOPLE GO

Go down, go down
Way down to Egypt land
Tell ol' Pharoah,
to let Julius and Ethel go.

THE CONDEMNED WRITES NEW SONGS

Who's afraid of the electric chair?
The electric chair,
the electric chair.
Who's afraid of the electric chair?
Fa-la-la-la-la.
They can shove it up their spine for all I care.
They can dump it in the Hudson for all I care.
Fa-la-la-la-la.

JULIE ARRIVES AT SING SING
MAY 16, 1951

Now in a cage in the men's wing.
Iron bars between us
will hold our silent kisses,
our silent embraces.

PLANTING THE SEED

We are not being executed today.
How long we have to live,
I don't know. I planted
an apple seed a few days ago.
I patiently water it, and the green
is bravely breaking through.

WHAT WE DO ABOUT THE BOYS

While we wait for the results of our appeals,
we discuss Michael and Robby with Manny.

We know him well enough now, we're in it deep enough
to call our lawyer by his first name.

Good news!
The boys are leaving that despicable Home.

In June, Julie's mother, Sophie, takes them in.
She has just rented an Upper Manhattan apartment

overlooking the Harlem River. I love her.
She shows no fear. And she adores her

grandsons. She makes them the chicken and fish
they like, real food, not garbage like hot dogs.

Michael and Robby share a bedroom at Bubbie Sophie's.
I pen long letters to Manny with instructions

for my boys. I'm still
their mother.

I AM THE MOST EXPENSIVE INMATE

JULY 1951

Hoo-hah!
The *Times* reported that I
am the most expensive inmate
at Sing Sing in its entire 126-year history.
I have cost the federal government
nearly three thousand dollars so far, mainly
because four matrons are assigned to me
and me alone.

REUNION DAY!
AUGUST 1951

I am wild to see my bunnies!
I haven't seen them in nearly a year.
Manny brings them to Sing Sing.
It is quite a trek, even once inside the prison.
They wait with Manny in a waiting area.
Then, when called for, they walk through
a large steel door and out into a yard.
There a van picks them up
and delivers them
to the Death House,
aka the CCs, or Condemned Cells.
More doors, flight of stairs.
Finally, they enter a bright, airy room
with a long table, many chairs,
with high windows and bars.

"Mommy, you're littler!"
And then they propose why,
and decide it's because I'm
wearing slippers and a housecoat,
instead of heels and a dress.
I've shrunk. I give them
all the hugs and kisses I've
stored up and I never want to let
them go.

I share an envelope
of carefully collected
and unusual insects with Robby. Dear
Julie thought of that. Robby
shrieks in delight. I hope
Julie can hear him in his cell
in the men's wing.

CURIOUS

My nine-year-old grills the guard:
Where is the electric chair?
Is it down that hallway there?
How does it work?
Can I see it?

I want to pull him
into my lap, onto
this sturdy chair.
Stroke his hair, play word games,
and keep him far away
from images he'd never
be able to forget.

THE WAR WITHIN

I withdraw into myself, all sides battling each other.
The world outside no longer exists.
I am much less afraid of the situation I'm in,
Though, I mourn the lack of your fervent kisses.

The world outside no longer exists.
The boys, our legal fight, fill my thoughts.
I mourn the lack of your fervent kisses.
You say our mental whoopee shows confidence.

The boys, our legal fight, fill my thoughts.
How can we plan when we don't know the future?
You say our mental whoopee shows confidence.
My persistence is wearing thin.

How can we plan when we don't know the future?
Though I know we still need to discuss legalities,
My persistence is wearing thin
As we still have a number of items to resolve.

Though I know we still need to discuss legalities,
And we must address the boys' future visits and upbringing,
We still have a number of items to resolve.
I withdraw into myself, all sides battling each other.

MY SECOND BIRTHDAY BEHIND BARS

SEPTEMBER 1951

I am now thirty-six
Surrounded by bars and cards
Sent by Julie, the boys,
Julie's family.

I pray my next birthday
will be in my own home
with cake and candles.

EACH LETTER I RECEIVE FROM MY BOYS

I picture them at kitchen tables,
words and ink spilling onto paper
under the watchful eyes of
      Aunt Lena
      Aunt Ethel.

I picture Michael and Robby in Bernie's car,
bundling in the back seat,
shuffling to Mama's,
then sitting at her kitchen table,
words and ink struggling onto paper
under her watchful eyes.

I picture them at Sophie's,
snuggling against each other,
telling each other everything will be all right.

REVERSAL EXPECTED

Though Manny and Julie assure me of our release,
a harmonica-rich blues song thrums inside me.

I write Julie to love only me; I am his wife,
giving him everything I've got.

We launch an appeal with Manny's arguments:
The death penalty violates the Eighth Amendment
Trial results were based on our beliefs, not our actions
Dovey and Ruth's testimonies were based on self-preservation.

REVERSAL DENIED

The U.S. Court of Appeals
upholds Judge Kaufman's conviction
and sentencing.

Manny shows us a copy
of the *Daily Worker*.
It says: We "were tried
by headlines and hysteria.
The fight to save the Rosenbergs
is the fight to keep America
free from Buchenwalds and Dachaus"—
Nazi concentration camps.

What does this mean? The fight
to save us is the fight to keep
America free from fascism.

MY BUNNIES ARE PRECIOUS TO ME

It plagues me the effect of our situation
on our bunnies. I write letter after letter
to Manny with detailed instructions
on how they should be raised. My
mother-in-law is wonderful, but
her health is failing and her helper
lacks the kind, consistent care
Michael and Robby need. I've contacted
a trusted child psychologist to straighten things out.

I must remember to order a box
of Schrafft's candy for the boys'
next visit.

THE WEIGHT OF EVERY LITTLE THING

I want to welcome my in-laws,
offer them coffee and cake,
slip on my apron and invite them
to stay for dinner.

Instead, we meet in prison, their bodies
searched before entering. Even a photograph
must be left behind at Sing Sing. A guard
will bring me the photograph after the visit.

No cups of coffee with cream and sugar,
stirred to perfection,
no pound cake or ice cream for dessert,
no folded napkins to catch any crumbs.

Instead, I catch crumbs of news from home,
devour them like the most expensive caviar,
not caring if I make a mess.

The visits from Lena, Ethel, Dave, and my brother Bernie
do not happen often enough to fill the spaces
between my prison bars. All must be planned
and approved ahead of time. Everyone leads
a busy life but me, unless one counts
endless letter-writing, fingers bleeding raw
from pressing hard on pencil stubs, not allowed
even the cheapest blue ballpoint pen.

THE FAIR FLOWER OF OSSINING MANOR
OCTOBER 1951

This fair flower (me) of Ossining Manor (Sing Sing prison)
manages to get through a tense
visit from brother Bernie.

This fair flower makes it hard for him,
he says, to keep the peace within the family.
He couldn't wait to get the bus out of here.

This fair flower of Ossining Manor
pines for her husband and visits
with her babies.

This fair flower of Ossining Manor
jots down answers in anticipation
of the boys' many questions.

This fair flower of Ossining Manor
lives in the spaces between iron bars
at Sing Sing.

WEDNESDAYS

When the new week starts,
I know Wednesday is not far behind.

On that day, I get to see my sweetheart,
in that no man's land between
the women's and men's cells. We
get to discuss our children,
get to breathe hope for our future,
cramming our lives into a single barred hour.

IN MY CELL

What is white?
    Sink
    Toilet paper
    Bed
    Metal head post
    Face towels
    Laundry soap
    Our innocence.

What is black?
    Metal bookcase
    Writing table
    Comb
    My trust in mankind.

What is red?
    Box of Colgate
    Toothbrush
    Lipstick
    Slurs and smears.

SNOW ANGELS

I used to love swiping my finger
along the icing on a birthday cake.

I now love to make initials
in the snow:
M.R., R.R., E.R., and J.R.

Oh, my angels, we are all melting.

DAYLIGHT SAVINGS TIME

More hours of recreation time
     and freedom of movement
More sunlight
     and Vitamin D
     and spring fever
More prisoner releases
     and room in the yard
More hope
     but steel cell walls
     my hands can't rip open.

WE DEMAND JUSTICE!
NOVEMBER 1951

Protests at Sing Sing gates
Petitions proclaiming our innocence
Press releases for rallies
Picket lines outside the White House
Public service announcements blasted from trucks.

Copies of the trial transcript for sale
to raise money for our cause through this new
National Committee to Secure Justice in the Rosenberg Case.

WHAT IT MEANS TO BE A MOTHER ON MOTHER'S DAY

MAY 11, 1951

I tack my children's colored drawings to the cell wall
Pretend the plastic bouquets of violets, pansies, and daffodils
   are real
Close my eyes so my lily-white bed looks and smells
   like a real garden.

Most of all, I close my eyes and remember
the way it used to be when real meant real
   when I could give my boys their bath
   when they closed their sweet eyes to sleep
   when Julie and I held each other in the night.

Some mothers pull their babies close to them
every day. But here in the CCs, I can only trace
their colored lines and photographed faces.

ETHEL ROSENBERG #110510

I write
letters to Julie #110649

I write
letters to my bunnies

I write
letters to Julie's sisters and brother

I write
letters to Manny

I set
deadlines for myself

I keep an eye
on the time for the daily post

I write
before they take my pencil for the night.

STUBBLE

At home, we use screens to keep out
undesirables—soot, insects, pigeons.

Here when we're allowed to visit,
a screen separates me from Julie.

I can see his stubble, feel his breath,
but I can't touch,

I can't kiss,
I can't hold.

We are in the same place
at the same time. And yet we aren't.

WHAT IT'S COME DOWN TO

Is a good pair of panties
that don't scratch or itch.

I ask Julie's sister
to please shop for me.

It's not much to ask for
as long as she can get

just the plain white variety
on sale at Lord & Taylor.

SATURDAY NIGHT CONCERT

When I hear Old Man Toscanini
on the NBC *Summer Symphony,*
I think of younger days when I sang in the choir,
the acoustics that fed my veins,
fueled my ambitions.

When I hear Toscanini,
I know there's a big world out there
full of Haydn, Strauss, and Stravinsky,
that one bow string can burst the walls
of Saturday nights.

When I hear the old man,
I immediately write Julie
and tell him that while Toscanini
carries me away, he alone is my savior.

THE TRIAL OF THE TRIAL RECORD

We, the Rosenbergs, cannot thank the National Committee
to Secure Justice in the Rosenberg Case
enough for giving Julie and me access
to our own trial transcript.

We, the Rosenbergs, are grateful
to the NCSJRC chapters
emerging in New York and throughout the country,
lending thousands of voices to our innocence.

We, the Rosenbergs, thank Manny Bloch
for his efforts to protect the record. He may
do as he wishes with our tome of
comments, disputes, and details.

We will not be angry if he does nothing.
We, the Rosenbergs, have unwittingly
become legal experts. We see
how politics leaves due process to hang.

HOW I HATE TO GET UP IN THE MORNING

Sleepless nights,
exhausting days—
how I hate to get up in the morning.

Newspaper lunacies,
Manny's lack of superpowers—
how I hate to get up in the morning.

So much left unsaid.
Unless it's Wednesday,
I hate to get up in the morning.

To mask each day
with pasted smile,
I tire of getting up in the morning.

NEW HOPE WITH A NEW PRESIDENT

Dwight Eisenhower, a Republican,
has just been elected President.
Julie writes to say this election,
a landslide,
shows America wants peace.
Eisenhower promises to end
the war in Korea.

With a new leader in place,
we have an opportunity.
Julie and I will make notes
for Manny to write
a petition to Eisenhower
to commute my sentence
or pardon me.
Julie insists on this.

CRY WOLF

Our new execution date
is fixed for the week
of January 12, 1953.

Like Prokofiev's *Peter and the Wolf*,
cry "wolf" enough and no one
will take notice when real danger lurks.

G-D IS PRESIDENT EISENHOWER: OUR PETITION
JANUARY 1953

We raise our song to Dwight, our Ike, our only hope.
Hear us, o Lord, grant us clemency.
Blessed is the United States forever and ever.
We love America and You with all we've got.
We swear to teach this love to our children
In our waking moments
In our sleeping moments.
We wear the stars and stripes on our foreheads
and not the hammer and sickle.
We are all for red, white, and blue.
Let us prove our American nature.
Let Your reign fall upon us in sheets of release.

MAMA VISITS FOR THE FIRST AND LAST TIME

JANUARY 21, 1953

It goes something like this:

"So what would have been so terrible
if you had backed up his story?"
meaning Dovey.

"What, and take the blame
for a crime I never committed,
and allow my name and my husband's,
and children's to be blackened
to protect him? What, and go along
with a story that I knew
to be untrue?"

"Yes, you got me straight. Lie."

That half-brother of mine, Sammy,
once wrote me:
"There is not much more
disgrace you could bring
to our family."

Do I need enemies
with a family like this?

DWIGHT "IKE" EISENHOWER IS NO PAL OF OURS
FEBRUARY 11, 1953

Ike!

Ike!

Ike!

Everybody wants Ike for president.

Everybody wants to put him in the White House.

Everybody wants to follow him, conform to his word.

But when we try, Ike slams the door on us,

refusing our petition for clemency.

Ike!

Ike!

Ike!

No, not everybody roots for Ike as president.

MOVING TARGET

New execution date:
week of March 8, 1953,
then June 15,
then June 18.
Is it gallows humor
that they chose
our fourteenth wedding anniversary
for our death?

WELCOME TO THE GAMBLING CASINO OF THE SUPREME COURT AND THE U.S. COURT OF APPEALS

FEBRUARY 17–MAY 25, 1953

For three months, the croupier of the courts spins the roulette wheel.

Red

       You're Soviet spies.

       You stole.

       You die.

       Appeal denied.

Black

       We're sorry.

       You're innocent.

       You live.

Julie, Manny, and I—no, the whole world—
watches the circular streak.
The cycles slow.
The spokes ready to catch the lever.

Just when we're certain
Black will win.
The court stomps its feet,
and the lever inches into Red.

Two out of three,
Three out of five

Denied.

THE FEDERAL DIRECTOR OF
THE BUREAU OF PRISONS VISITS
JUNE 2, 1953

We can get clemency if we talk.
My life can be saved if I talk against Julie.

Julie and I issue a press release,
insisting on our innocence
once again.

A RUSH TO THE FINISH

The Supreme Court grants us a final stay!
Two days later it is revoked,
our seventh denial.
Though there were dissenting opinions,
the Court did not find enough substantial reason
to suspend the death sentence.
Manny files a second petition
with President Eisenhower.
Much shorter
Much tighter.
We state that if we die, the guilt will be America's.
Denied.
We will be sitting for our new electric
portraits tonight.